THE YEAR COMES ROUND

Haiku through the Seasons

Sid Farrar

Illustrated by **Ilse Plume**

www.av2books.com

Your AV² Media Enhanced book gives you a fiction readalong online. Log on to www.av2books.com and enter the unique book code from this page to use your readalong.

AV² Readalong Navigation

Go to www.av2books.com, and enter this book's unique code.

BOOK CODE

Y599073

AV² by Weigl brings you media enhanced books that support active learning.

First Published by

ALBERT WHITMAN & COMPANY

Publishing children's books since 1919

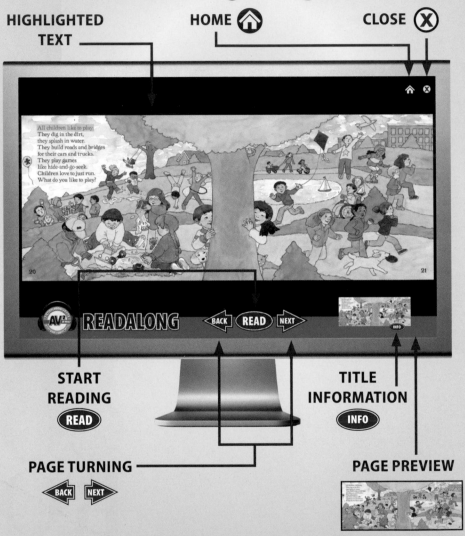

Published by AV² by Weigl
350 5th Avenue, 59th Floor New York, NY 10118
Websites: www.av2books.com   www.weigl.com

Copyright ©2015 AV² by Weigl

Printed in the United States of America in North Mankato, Minnesota
1 2 3 4 5 6 7 8 9 0 18 17 16 15 14

042014
WEP080414

Library of Congress Control Number: 2014938423

ISBN 978-1-4896-2425-3 (hardcover)
ISBN 978-1-4896-2426-0 (single user eBook)
ISBN 978-1-4896-2427-7 (multi-user eBook)

Text copyright ©2012 by Sid Farrar.
Illustrations copyright ©2012 by Ilse Plume.
Published in 2012 by Albert Whitman & Company.

THE YEAR COMES ROUND

Haiku through the Seasons

4

Each windowpane's a
masterpiece, personally
signed: Your Friend, Jack Frost

Snowmen stand very
still, hoping the noon sun won't
notice they are there

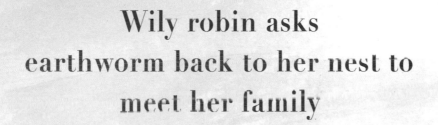

Wily robin asks
earthworm back to her nest to
meet her family

The morning rain bursts
dandelions from the earth like
countless little suns

Surprised by her new
webbed feet, tadpole considers
a career on shore

Like tiny fallen
stars, fireflies quietly blink
their secrets at dusk

Thick, black clouds grumble
at giving up water to
the parched earth below

A mystery how
these endless rows of corn can
agree on their height

19

Apples loll beneath
emptying branches, dreaming
cider and hot pie

Waiting patiently
in the pumpkin patch for his
face: Jack O' Lantern

Lawns call a truce with
mowers and slip beneath their
white blankets to sleep

Brown bear politely
offers to surrender his
den to nosy skunk

HAIKU

Haiku (pronounced "hi KOO") is a form of poetry.

A haiku is made up of just three lines, with five syllables in the first line, seven in the second, and five again in the third. (A syllable is the smallest unit we hear when we sound out the parts of a word—for example, hai-ku has two syllables.)

Haiku are almost always about the natural world and usually are set in a season or month of the year. Haiku also use nature images to depict the changes in the four seasons over the year.

The haiku in this book follow the twelve months that make up each year according to the Gregorian calendar, which is commonly used around the world today.

The first recorded haiku date back to eighteenth century Japan.

THE CYCLE OF LIFE

A year is the time it takes for the earth to go around the sun. The earth is the third planet from the sun and orbits it every 365 to 366 days, the number of days in a year. At the same time that the earth is circling the sun, it also spins around once every twenty-four hours, which is how we measure a day.

Long before we used today's twelve-month calendar, people marked the passage of time by the change of seasons—winter, spring, summer, and fall. The seasons are experienced differently on different parts of the planet. People north of the equator, the imaginary line around the middle of the earth, get to enjoy more dramatic changes in the weather, flora, and fauna than people in the mostly warmer southern hemisphere.

The haiku in this book depict little vignettes in the natural world to describe these changes across the seasons and months of the year.

WINTER

Winter begins in late December and lasts through early March in the northern hemisphere. That is when precipitation and air moisture turn to ice and snow as the air temperature falls below freezing. Ice can form on plants and on smooth surfaces like the glass in windows where patterns of crystals can take magical shapes, such as the storied sprite that came to be called Jack Frost. As the snow begins to melt, often with warmer days starting in late February and early March, the birds that had migrated south in the fall return to their summer homes and begin to look for food to feed their young.

SPRING

As April arrives, the snow turns mostly to rain, alternating with bright sunlit days that grow longer as May turns to June. Leaves appear on trees and plants spring up and flower from the seeds that have found fertile soil on forest floors, prairies, and lawns. Eggs that fish and frogs have laid in underwater weeds hatch and swim to the surface of lakes and ponds, looking for food. Tadpoles lose their tails and grow legs that carry them onto the shore where they breathe air as mature frogs. By the end of June, insects have filled the air—bees dance, butterflies flutter, and fireflies blink their bellies—looking for food and mates to carry on the next generation.

SUMMER

July days are often the longest and hottest of the year. When clouds become heavy enough with water to produce rain, there can be violent storms with electric discharges resulting in lightning. In turn, lightning causes the disturbance in the air that we hear as thunder. The rain nourishes the soil in fields now filled with maturing crops like oats, wheat, and corn that had been planted in spring and that will be harvested in fall. In September, harvest of crops such as fruit trees begins. Fruit not harvested will fall to the ground and, along with the stalks and vines left behind in farmers' fields, will decay and add nutrients to the soil, enriching it for new growth in spring the following year.

FALL

The harvesting of many crops such as corn, soybeans, and pumpkins generally happens in October. Days cool and shorten and, with the exception of evergreens, the leaves of many trees and bushes turn various shades of orange, red, yellow, and brown and fall off. As October turns to November, birds and Monarch butterflies fly back to the warmth of the South, and rain turns to snow. Fields and lawns, now brown and covered with fallen leaves, turn white as snow deepens, and many animals store food and seek shelter from the cold—some settling into dens for a winter's sleep.

Earth circles the sun
spinning a tapestry of
days, months, seasons—life.